Mr. Potato Head

ACROSS AMERICA

All rights reserved.
Printed in Hong Kong
ISBN 0-525-45553-1

First Edition
10 9 8 7 6 5 4 3 2 1

Mr. Potato Head® ★ ACROSS AMERICA ★

Written by Nancy Shayne and Laura Kightlinger
Illustrated by Tom Platoni

PLAYSKOOL BOOKS

Playskool Books®
an imprint of Dutton Children's Books, a division of Penguin USA

Mr. Potato Head looked out the window of his little house in Pawtucket, Rhode Island, which stood not far from the factory where he was born. He thought for sure he had seen someone put a letter in his mailbox.

Mr. Potato Head didn't usually receive much mail.

"Well, I'm going to go outside and get it," he thought. "That's what people do. No point in sitting here wondering what it could be."

The postmark on the envelope said:

IDAHO

Mr. Potato Head opened the envelope and read the fancy card that fell out.

"I can't believe my eyes!" he said, delighted. "A Potato Head family reunion! I haven't been to Idaho in years, and I've never been to a family reunion. In fact," he said quite seriously, "I've hardly been anywhere at all. I think it's time for me to hit the road!"

"There are only two weeks before the reunion. I'd better get going!" Mr. Potato Head went inside to pack.

"Let's see," he said. "What do I need to bring so I can peel out of here? I'll need a guitar and my surfboard, a jacket, some eyes, a nose, a raincoat, a bunch of ears, and a sturdy pair of shoes. Wow! This suitcase is going to be heavy. I'd better take an extra hand."

When Mr. Potato Head found out that the next bus out of town would be leaving in twenty minutes, he decided to wait at the diner.

"My goodness," said Mr. Potato Head, sipping his coffee and looking at the map he had brought along. "There are more places between here and Idaho than I thought. I wonder how many of them I'll have time to see. And which direction should I head in first?"

Mr. Potato Head soon finished his cup of coffee, but he still had to wait a little longer. To pass the time, he counted to one hundred.

"One potato, two potato, three potato . . ."

Finally the bus pulled up to the curb. The bus driver opened the doors and smiled at Mr. Potato Head in a friendly way. She said, "Hello! I'll bet you're going to Idaho."

"How did you know?" Mr. Potato Head was astonished but pleased.

"I could tell by your expression. Is there anyplace else you'd like to see before we get there?" the bus driver asked.

"I'd like to see America," said Mr. Potato Head.

"Okay," she said. "Heads up, America! Here we come!"

Mr. Potato Head stowed his suitcase in the luggage compartment. He was so excited that he almost left his arm with it.

"First stop... Niagara Falls!"
the bus driver announced.

Mr. Potato Head couldn't
wait to get out.

"Good thing I packed my
raincoat," he said to himself.
"There's nothing slicker than
a wet potato skin. I wonder
if this suitcase floats? I want
to get a closer look at those
falls."

"Gosh!" said Mr. Potato Head. "New York really is the Big Apple! Look at the Statue of Liberty! Wasn't she the one who said, 'Give me your tired, your hungry, your potatoes'? She holds up her torch like this—Oops! There goes my ice cream."

Then Mr. Potato Head grew thoughtful. "My great-grand-potatoes arrived in Manhattan on a boat from Ireland, just like this one, a long time ago. I wish I could have met my great-grandfather. Now *he* was the real potato!"

"A lot of my relatives come from farms," said Mr. Potato Head. "They're not all city potatoes like me, you know. I love the smell of horses and cows."

Mr. Potato Head wiped his forehead. The sun was hot. "It was nice of that farmer to lend me his hat. I'm sure I felt my ears getting sunburned. I'd better change them when I get back on the bus!"

"**I** hope it's not too dark to take a picture," said Mr. Potato Head to himself. "What a beautiful house! This is where the president of the whole country lives. It's very nice of him to let me visit. I'm sure he must be busy."

Mr. Potato Head frowned. "I wonder if he's ever been to my house? I can't remember. I'd better be polite and invite him again."

"**W**hoa!" said Mr. Potato Head. "Come back here, baseball cap! The Cape Canaveral Anti-Gravity chamber sure works. I wonder how astronauts keep their eyes and ears and hands on. It must be a real problem for them when they're trying to work the control panels!"

logical Site

JOHN F. KENNE
SPACE CENTER
Spaceport U.S.A.
(Visitors Center)
CAPE CANA
AIR FORCE
Cape Cana
Cape Canaveral
rritt Island
Cocoa Beach
Patrick Air Force b
Satellite Beach
Indian Harbour
Canova Beach
Melbourne

"**L**ook! There's the St. Louis Arch," Mr. Potato Head exclaimed. "Ever since I was a new potato, I've wanted to ride a riverboat down the Mississippi. This is a very popular attraction for tourists. I'm lucky I made it on board by my skin and my teeth.

"Riding down here near the water isn't bad at all. Let's just hope my arm stays on!"

Mr. Potato Head enjoyed being in Kansas.

"Corn! Corn! Corn!" he cheered. "I'm up to my ears in corn, and that's no joke."

It was very windy when Mr. Potato Head got off the bus in Yellowstone Park. Old Faithful decided to borrow Mr. Potato Head's suitcase. But she gave it back. He knew she would.

"That's why she's called Old Faithful," he told the bus driver. "I'm glad I got it back. I have a tendency to lose things!"

"**H**ello!" cried Mr. Potato Head when he got to Mount Rushmore. But nobody answered except the echo. "Hello-o-o-o-o . . ."

"These faces are not as friendly as mine," Mr. Potato Head remarked. "But maybe it's not their fault. Maybe no one made smiling mouths for them to wear. And I've got some to spare!"

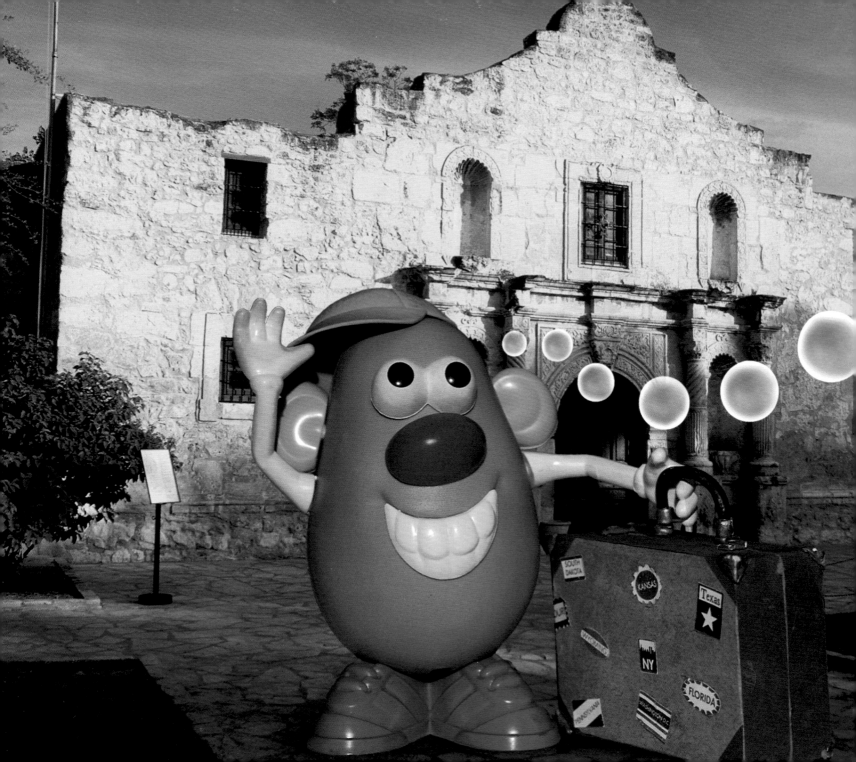

"**I** remember the Alamo," said Mr. Potato Head. He was proud of all the brave potatoes who had fought to make Texas a state. For one, there was his great-great-uncle, Gravy Croquette, the famous frontier spud.

"Uncle Gravy always wore a coonskin cap," said Mr. Potato Head. "I'm going to see if I can buy one at the souvenir shop!"

"**W**ow!" said Mr. Potato Head. "It's a long way down to the bottom of the Grand Canyon. I'd better not lean over too far! When I get dizzy, I tend to lose my head. And if I lose it here, I might never find it again."

When Mr. Potato Head got to Hollywood, he thought no one would recognize him in his sunglasses. But almost as soon as he got off the bus, he was swarmed by a crowd of fans and reporters. "California sure is friendly!" he said happily.

Next he went to a special sidewalk, where he wrote his name in the concrete. Then he took off his hands and feet and pressed them into the cement. Next thing he knew, they had disappeared! Somebody had taken them as souvenirs. "Good thing I packed some extras," said Mr. Potato Head.

Mr. Potato Head next decided to fly to Alaska. When he got there, he changed into his blue lips and ears and went for a dogsled ride. But when he told the dogs to turn around, they looked confused. "I guess they don't speak potato," said Mr. Potato Head. "Or maybe they think I should be ahead instead of behind them!"

"It sure is fun hanging eight in Hawaii," said Mr. Potato Head. "I never knew surfing was such a breeze. I always thought it would be awfully hard to keep your feet on — I mean, keep on your feet. And tonight I'm going to dance the hula at the luau! This is the life."

When Mr. Potato Head got off the bus in Idaho, he was very excited to read the sign that was posted by the road. "Look!" he said. "Ten million and one! I guess that means my Cousin Tuber had her baby already."

The sun was so hot and the grass looked so inviting that Mr. Potato Head couldn't wait to take off his shoes. Then he waved good-bye to the bus driver, who was already pulling away. "See you next week for the ride home!" She honked.

POTATO POPULATION: TEN MILLION and 1

WELCOME
TO
IDAHO

PULL HERE

Mr. Potato Head's whole family came running out to meet him. Crazy Uncle Scallop, Aunt Frenchie, Grandma and Grandpa Au Gratin, and even the tots. They all were wearing their very best outfits. Mr. Potato Head had lost most of his extra parts during his trip, but nobody seemed to mind.

It was a magical moment,
and luckily the official
Potato Head Family Reunion
photographer was right there.

When Mr. Potato Head got back to his house in Pawtucket, he began to unpack all his parts and possessions. Each one reminded him of something. And his suitcase was covered with stickers.

"I guess nobody can call me a stay-at-home potato now," he said proudly. "We potatoes are very versatile. I seemed to fit in everywhere I went. And, best of all, I had a great time!"

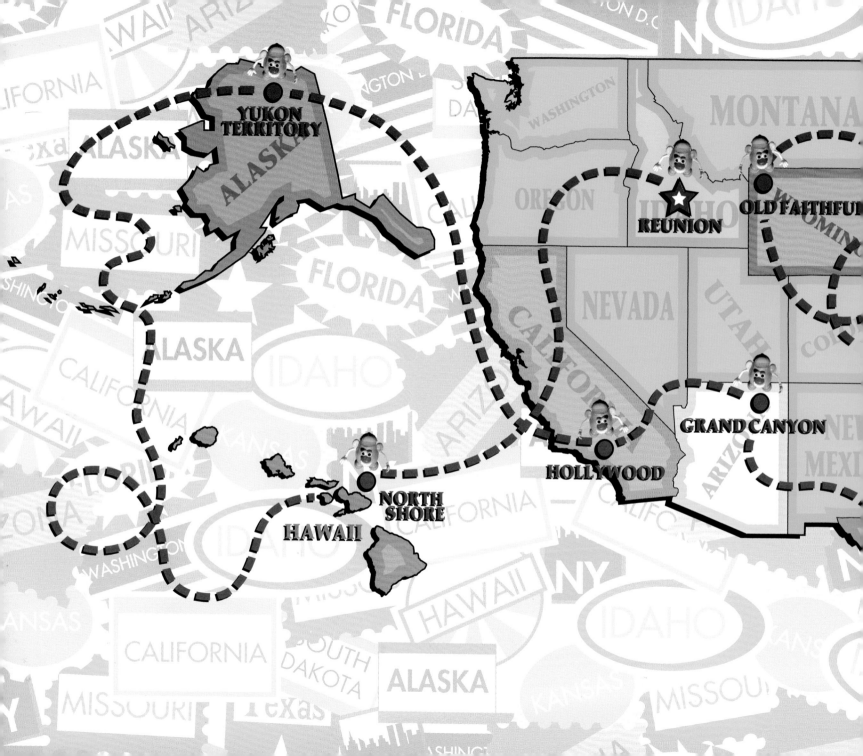

MASSACHUSETTS

PAWTUCKET, RHODE ISLAND (HOME)

NIAGARA FALLS

AMISH COUNTRY

CONNECTICUT

STATUE OF LIBERTY
NEW JERSEY

WASHINGTON, D.C.
DELAWARE

MARYLAND

CORN COUNTRY

ST. LOUIS

ALAMO

CAPE CANAVERAL